George William Lasher

The Gospel in Cuba

The story of Díaz - a marvel of modern missions

George William Lasher

The Gospel in Cuba
The story of Díaz - a marvel of modern missions

ISBN/EAN: 9783337380861

Printed in Europe, USA, Canada, Australia, Japan

Cover: Foto ©Andreas Hilbeck / pixelio.de

More available books at **www.hansebooks.com**

THE

STORY OF DIAZ

A Marvel of Modern Missions

BY

GEORGE WILLIAM LASHER, D. D.

CINCINNATI

GEO. E. STEVENS

1893.

MAP OF CUBA.

CARIBBEAN
GULF OF MEXICO
STRAITS OF FLORIDA
GREAT BAHAMA BANK
GULF OF BATABANO
ISLA DE PINOS

SCALE OF MILES.

TO

WILLIAM J. NORTHEN, L.L. D.,

THE CONSCIENTIOUS EDUCATOR,

THE INTELLIGENT AGRICULTURIST,

THE CHRISTIAN GOVERNOR,

This Sketch of the Apostle of Cuba
is Respectfully Dedicated,

.

IN MEMORY OF DELIGHTFUL ASSOCIATIONS

ENJOYED DURING A TRIP TO

"THE QUEEN OF THE ANTILLES,"

IN 1893.

"The sons also of them that afflicted thee shall come bending unto thee; and all they that despised thee shall bow themselves down at the soles of thy feet; and they shall call thee The city of the Lord, The Zion of the Holy One of Israel." *Isaiah, lx.,* 14.

"He shall not fail nor be discouraged, till he have set judgment in the earth; and the isles shall wait for his law." *Isaiah, xlii.,* 4.

THE STORY OF DIAZ.

ALBERTO JOSE DIAZ was born in 1852, the oldest of twenty-four children born to one mother, who was married at the age of twelve years, and is now in good health, a most valuable and hearty coadjutor of her son and the other members of her family. His father was a pharmaceutist, living in Guanabacoa, a town of some 17,000 inhabitants, just across the bay to the eastward of Havana. After a good education in the schools of his native town, Alberto became a student in the University of Havana; he, after graduating, studied medicine in the same city, and, in due time, was admitted to practice as a physician. Though his father was not rich, the education of the son was accomplished at a cost of $9,000, continuing through twelve years.

(5)

A PATRIOT.

Not long after his graduation and admittance to the practice of medicine, a rebellion against the tyrannous rule of the Spaniards broke out, and patriotism sent the young doctor to the camp of the rebels. He was made a captain of cavalry, and was soon in the field, helping to break the Spanish yoke which had become intolerable, but which was more closely bound upon the necks of the Cubans than they had supposed. Perhaps their own method of fastening the yoke upon their oxen may be the best illustration of the binding of the Spanish yoke upon the necks of the Cubans. The yoke of the ox is not fitted to his neck, but to his head, just back of and over his horns, and the fastening is with ropes so wound about the horns, and reinforced by a ring in the nose (from which a rope passes over the head), that the creature is utterly helpless. He can not move his head a quarter of an inch in any direction, save up and down, and the weight of the burden upon the yoke bows the nose to within three or four inches of the ground. A more pitiable sight is rarely met with than a yoke of Cuban oxen attached to one of their huge and ungainly carts. But the yoke of Spain is no less grievous than is that ox-yoke. Twenty thousand soldiers are quartered on the people, and the expense of supporting them, together with the other revenues required by Spain, imposes a tax of $27,000,000 annually upon one and a half million of people. What wonder that Cubans are restive? What wonder that they are, as they have been for many generations, ready to seize every opportunity which gives any hope of success in rebellion? And so it was that the young Cuban physician found himself among the patriots of his native island, trying to drive out the Spaniards.

AT SEA ON A LOG.

One afternoon, while he was on duty, he was sent ahead of his command, with a companion, to find a suitable spot for an encampment. While thus engaged, the two men were cut out by Spanish troopers, and found themselves in danger of immediate capture, or death. They rode their horses hurriedly into a thicket, and, springing from their saddles, plied the whip to the loosened animals, driving them out of reach, in hope that

the Spaniards would go after the horses and
forget the riders. They were on a point of
land running out into the sea on the southern
coast. Instead of following the horses, the
Spaniards chose to find the men, if possible;
but, as the shades of night were gathering
around them, they determined to encamp and
keep the rebels on the point all night, and
then take them in the morning. The young
men had seen enough of Spanish treatment of
prisoners to know that their lives were worth
but little to them, if they were caught. So,
during the night, they procured a plank, and,
knowing that a current was sweeping along
the coast, they thought to get into it and
thus be borne beyond the Spanish lines to a
place where they might land in safety. But
when morning came they were far out of
reach of land, and unable to reach the shore.

IN A STRANGE CITY.

It was a very sorry prospect that opened
to them, when the sun came up and its rays
beat down upon them. No food, no water
for their thirst, no possibility of reaching
shore. Soon they were seized with cramps;
one of them fell off the plank and was

drowned; Diaz became unconscious, and in that condition was picked up by a fishing-boat, and was, soon after, placed upon a vessel bound for New York where, in due time, he arrived, a stranger and penniless, in a great city. He had some knowledge of the cigar business, and, if he could not make cigars, he could find fellow-country-men in the cigar shops. These he sought, and soon he had made an engagement to become the reader for the shop. The custom in the cigar shop, since the work is of a quiet character, is to fix up an elevated seat and employ some one who can read well to sit up there and read to the workmen while they ply their trade. In this way they listen not only to the news of the day, but often to novels of a not very pure character, and to books of a far from elevating tone. But it is a pastime, to listen while they work. Diaz was a reader, and thus he got his living, while, in his odd hours, he thought to perfect his knowledge of medicine, giving special attention to the treatment of the eye. He went to a medical school where the eye was specially treated, and put himself under the instruction of a physician whom he came to regard highly, and who

also became interested in his pupil. But
he could speak almost no word of English,
though he had learned to read it a little.

SICK UNTO DEATH.

Meantime, he had found a boarding place
in Brooklyn, where were also several other
boarders, strangers to him, none of them able
to converse with him. Not long after becoming settled in his boarding house, he was
attacked with pneumonia; and soon after the
physician pronounced it a bad case, and gave
the opinion that it would prove fatal. One
morning the keeper of the boarding house
came to the table and said to her boarders:
"That young Cuban whom you have seen
here at the table is going to die. He has
pneumonia, and the doctor gives no hope of
his recovery." Among those who listened to
the announcement was Miss Alice Tucker, a
Christian young woman, whose heart was
touched, and whose thought went immediately out in behalf of his soul. She could
not allow that young man to die under the
same roof with herself, a stranger in a strange
city, and not do something for the salvation
of his soul.

But what could she do? She could not speak his language, and he could not understand hers. This she could do and would do; she could take her Testament and go up to his room and there pray for him. Possibly God would use something she might do for the salvation of the sick man. She took a little red-covered Testament and went up to his room and sat down by his bedside. She opened the Testament and read aloud several passages of Scripture; and then, putting her hand over her eyes, she prayed with silent but moving lips for a divine blessing upon the truth and upon the sufferer. He looked at her in amazement. Why did she read from that little book? Why did she seem to talk to herself? He was able to write a few words which he could not pronounce. He wrote on a slip of paper: "What is that book which you are reading?" She wrote in reply: "The New Testament — Bible." He wrote again: "What makes you talk to yourself?" She wrote in reply: "I am praying for you."

A NEW THOUGHT.

It was a new thought to him. He was familiar with the ways of the priests of Rome,

the confessional, the masses, etc.; but that
any one should pray thus, apart from a cruci-
fix, apart from a priest, apart from a church;
and that a young woman should pray for
him—what · did it mean? He had thought
that she was crazy, and therefore was talking
to herself. Now he was hardly more enlight-
ened as to her object. But he was not there
to die. He began to mend, and soon he was
able to go back to his companions and to his
preceptor in the medical school. To these
he began to tell the story of his sickness, and
of the conduct of the young woman. He
had asked her for the little book, and here it
was. It was the New Testament in English.
He had turned its pages with the deepest
interest, but could make very little out of it.
He spelled out words and then tried to turn
them into Spanish, if perchance he might
understand them better thus. He could make
but little progress; but one said to him:
"Why, you can get just such a book as that
in Spanish, by going up to the Bible House
at Ninth street and Fourth avenue." Could
he? Well, then he would have one; and
soon he had it. But he kept the little red
Testament in English, and treasures it as

a memento of the days of his blindness, when the grace of God was vouchsafed to him.

Diaz and his Testament became constant companions. He studied it with an ardent desire to know its contents. Especially was he interested in the narratives of the miracles of our Lord. When he came to that of the blind man whose eyes were anointed with the clay, he was especially affected by the exhibition of power. He himself was studying the eye, and how to cure blindness was a matter of the deepest interest to him. But here was a man who could cure blindness by a means which, in the hands of an ordinary practitioner, would rather injure the eye than cure its blindness. He talked with his preceptor in the medical college, a Christian man, an elder in a Presbyterian Church; but, both because of the language and because of the nature of the subject, he could get but little help. His teacher was interested in him and tried to help him into the truth; but without success.

A BLIND SINNER.

One day he came to the story of the healing of Bartimeus, at Jericho. Here was another wonderful display of power to give

sight to the blind. When Bartimeus had
been admonished to hold his peace, he cried
yet the more; and when Jesus stood still and
commanded him to be called, the blind man
hasted, cast away his garment and came to
Jesus. It was this passage which was blessed
to the conviction of the sinner. As Diaz read
it, he was moved by the thought—"I too am
a blind man ; and what is distressing about
it is that I can not see him who is able to heal
me." Thus, for the first time, he came to see
himself a blind sinner in need of salvation.
Standing face to face with the story of Bartimeus, he learned that he was helpless, unable
to save himself, unable to see Him who could
save him   Then he began to pray; to seek
salvation. It was a new way, and no one was
able to help him in it.   How long he groped
along that rugged, treacherous path we have
not been told ; and it is doubtful if he himself knows.   He talked with his teacher in
the college, but he got little good, though he
got sympathy.   All we know and all that he
knows is that he finally came into the light,
and could say, as he has been ever since able
to say :   "Whereas I was blind, now I see."
He came to see that Jesus is "the Light of

the world," and that he who believes in
Jesus doth not walk in darkness, but enjoys
the light of life. Immediately he began to
feel an ardent desire for the salvation of his
fellows, and soon was trying to tell them
what he had found in Christ Jesus. He had
attended no church, had listened to no ser-
mon, to no preacher. He knew nothing
about Protestant denominations. He was a
stranger in the great cities ; but he knew the
Lord Jesus Christ. With Him he came to be
on terms of intimate friendship. His fellows
were interested, so far that they would listen
to him; but we do not know that any of them
came to see Jesus as he saw him.

RETURNS TO CUBA.

After a time, the rebellion having been entirely put down, it seemed good to Spain to
declare amnesty to those who had not been
made prisoners, especially to those who had
fled their country ; and it seemed good to
Diaz to return to Havana and engage in the
practice of his profession, but especially to
carry to his former friends the gospel of the
grace of God which he had come to rejoice
in. He went, and soon had a considerable

practice. He went to his old friends of the University and the medical school, and began to tell them about the way of life as set forth in the New Testament. He carried the same gospel to the sick, his patients. He treated them for ailments of the body and ailments of the soul at the same time. But he had not been long engaged thus when his practice all at once left him. He had no patients. And he soon learned that the priests had got on his track. They had learned what he was doing among the sick, and they told the people that they were committing a great sin and imperilling their souls by having that man treat them. He was a heretic, and if they did not cease to receive his visits they need not expect Christian burial. What could he do? He was utterly helpless. He would go back to New York and see what he could do there. Perhaps the way would open for him to become useful in some other way.

AGAIN IN BROOKLYN.

He went to New York, to Brooklyn. His father, finding his position uncomfortable, though the rebellion had been quelled, came

also to New York, with his entire family,
thinking to make it his home, and found a
place of abode in Brooklyn, not far from
the Gethsemane Baptist church, Willoughby
Avenue. The Sabbath-school of that Church
was active, and before long the sisters, one
in her teens, the other much younger, were
induced and permitted to attend the school.
There they came under the influence of faithful teachers, and, though they could understand the language very imperfectly, yet
they soon began to get ideas, and these began
to take root in their hearts. They loved the
Sabbath-school, and saw that there was something taught there which they had never
dreamed of before; something which was of
vital interest to them. The older, Minnie,
became so much attached to the school and
to her teacher that she could not be kept away.
She talked with her brother, and began to
catch ideas from him. Soon after, the health
of the mother demanded that they return to
Cuba. It was arranged that the two girls
should remain with Alberto, for a time, and
the father consented to the arrangement "on
one condition." He said to his son: "Alberto,
we will leave the girls with you here, on one

condition: you must not try to make a Protestant of Minnie." Alberto readily promised; "for," says he, "I knew that Minnie had got so far along on the road to Protestantism that she did not need me to persuade her. She could not be stopped." So the parents went back to Cuba.

BAPTIZED.

After the parents had gone, leaving the daughters behind with their brother, he and Minnie went, one night, up to the Calvary Baptist church, in New York, where they witnessed a baptism performed by the Rev. Dr. MacArthur. As they looked and saw what was done, Minnie turned to her brother and said: "Alberto, that is just what it says in that little book, the Testament." And they agreed that it was so. The baptism was according to their understanding of what they read in the New Testament. They needed no argument, no explanation, to enable them to understand that. Not long after, Minnie, having attracted the attention of her teacher, and having come to give evidence of regeneration and of faith in Christ, applied for membership in the Gethsemane Baptist Church, was received and baptized, in October, 1882, by the highly esteemed pastor, the Rev. R. B. Montgomery, whose record is as follows : "Ten years ago last October, I was privileged to baptize Miss Minnie Diaz, then a member of my Sunday-school. One month later, November 26, I baptized Alberto J. Diaz, her brother, now the apostle of Cuba. Their experiences of the saving grace of God, though told in very broken English, were most satisfactory to all who heard them. They were lovingly received into fellowship."

And so it came about that Minnie gave her heart to Christ and was baptized—the first of the family, the first of all the Cubans. That was a little more than ten years ago. Now she is a most efficient helper of her brother, a teacher in a school, organist in the religious services of the church, and ready for anything which may seem to demand her help.

A LITTLE PROTESTANT.

Meantime, the younger sister, Clotilde, was in the same Sabbath-school, and when their brother took them both back with him to Havana, their mother greeted them with affection, but was shocked to learn that Minnie had become a Baptist. What could she do? If she could not prevent Minnie's becoming a Protestant, she could yet control Clotilde. So, when she put the child to bed, she would have her cross herself and say her "Hail Mary." But it was too late. The Bible and the instruction of a faithful Sabbath-school teacher had done their work. Clotilde refused to make the sign of the cross, or to pray to the Virgin. Her mother was greatly shocked and chagrined. Finally she said to the little girl, "If you do not make the sign of the cross, I will not kiss you good night."

"Very well, mother. I can't make the sign of the cross. It is not right. Good night, mother."

And the mother was obliged to leave the little Protestant to herself and her Savior. In process of time she gave evidence of genuine conversion, and was baptized by her brother in the presence of her delighted mother, who had herself been already baptized.

WHAT NEXT?

Now, having gone another step in his Christian career, having publicly " put on " the Lord Jesus Christ, the heart of Diaz began to turn again towards his native island. He became more bold in his profession, more sure of his ground. He began to feel a more ardent desire to tell his countrymen, more especially his old associates, what he had found in Christ. He talked with his pastor, and then he went over to New York, sought out Dr. Morehouse, of the Home Mission Society, and talked with him about the expediency and feasibility of opening a mission in Cuba. All he desired was some kind of backing, and he would go and carry the gospel to his fellow countrymen.

But Dr. Morehouse could not see his way clear to project a mission among the Romanists of Cuba. The Home Mission Society had its hands more than full. Cries were coming up from all parts of our own land for help to build churches, to support schools, to aid feeble churches, to support missionaries. The people were slow to respond to his appeals. They could not see the need of giving so much money to home missions. Some were indifferent, some were stingy, some were only half-hearted. The funds of the Society did not warrant the undertaking of a mission to Cuba. Diaz got no encouragement there. And Secretary Morehouse was not at fault. He acted up to the best light he had. He was going as fast as his brethren enabled him to go ; faster than some of them, thought he ought to go.

A BIBLE COLPORTEUR.

Just then there came to Diaz the announcement that a Female Bible Society in Philadelphia had thought of sending a colporteur to Cuba. They had heard that the island was open, as it had never been before. If they only had " the right man," they would send him. The right man was ready to undertake the work, and soon he was under appointment. In 1883 he went back to Cuba, taking his sisters with him.

It was then that his mother learned that Minnie had been baptized, and then also she found that the little Clotilde had imbibed so much Protestantism that she could not be induced to make the sign of the cross or pray to the Virgin. When Alberto landed in

Havana, as he says of himself, he had " nothing in the world but his box of Bibles and his faith in God." He was practically alone, laying siege to the Romanism of Cuba —one lone colporteur against a million and a half of Romanists. But, on his side was the Bible, Christ, the power of God, the promise, "Lo, I am with you always." On their side was superstition, idolatry, priest-craft, wickedness. He sat down before the fortress. No, he did not sit down. He went to work. He went out among the neighboring towns. He talked Christ and salvation. He sold Bibles, gave away Bibles.

The priests sometimes tell us that the Bible is not prohibited to the people ; that they are not forbidden to read it. But, though it may be true that some are permitted to read it, when they are of such standing that they can not be safely forbidden, there are two reasons why the Spanish-speaking Cubans can not and do not read the Spanish version of the Bible issued by the Church of Rome : One is that many of them can not read ; and the other, that no edition of the Bible in the Spanish language can be procured for less than $28, unless it be that published by the

American or some other Bible Society. Now,
however, the Bible in Spanish issued by the
American Bible Society is sold for 65 cents,
and the Rev. A. J. McKim told the writer
that, during the eight years since he became
colporteur, succeeding Bro. Diaz, he has sold
17,000 copies of the Bible, or Testament, in
Cuba.

IN PRISON.

Diaz entered upon his work as Bible colporteur with great zeal. It was precisely the
work for which his heart yearned. It gave
him opportunity to talk of Christ and salvation; to compare the teachings of Scripture
and that of the Church of Rome.

First of all, he went to his old associates,
in the university, the medical school, the
army—those to whom he had begun to tell
the story of salvation while he was yet a
novice. Now he was strong. He had not
only his faith in God, in Christ, in the Bible,
but he had the backing of the Bible Society.
One day he went out some distance from
Havana by rail, having two boxes of books
with him. He was not unknown to the
police. He had been a rebel, and the Span-

ish police was on the alert for any signs of
conspiracy against the government. When
they saw the former rebel with his boxes,
they thought of a possible conspiracy and
dynamite. As he was sitting in the car, an
officer tapped him on the shoulder and
asked: " Is your name Diaz?" " Yes, that
is my name." " I am to arrest you." And
he took the Bible man and his boxes of
Bibles to the nearest prison, and made his
report to the mayor of the town. The pris-
oner was put in one cell, and his boxes of
Bibles into another.

After he had been locked up, an officer
came and asked if he was a citizen of the
United States; and when Diaz answered that
he was, the officer made a note of the fact,
and Diaz wrote to the American consul for
that District, a Mr. Barger. On the following Sabbath he asked the jailer if he might
talk to the prisoners, and was refused the
privilege. But he wanted to tell them about
Jesus; so he sang a song, prayed aloud, took
a text and preached, so that all could hear
him, and all who could do so gathered about
his cell to listen. On Tuesday his friends
came with an order from the consul and re-

leased him. Then he took his boxes and went to a hotel and opened them. All wanted some of the filibustering books, so that he sold them all—one of them to the mayor. The next week the mayor came to him saying, "That is a good book," and asked him: "Where is infant baptism taught in the book?" Diaz told him it was not there. Then he asked: "Where is purgatory taught in the book?" and he was told that it was not there. Then Diaz told that mayor about Jesus, and subsequently baptized him, his jailer and seventy-five more citizens of that place. The mayor told him that the priests had informed against him and had been the cause of his imprisonment, though it was done under the plea that he might be a filibuster.

A RELIGIOUS SOCIETY.

But his work centered in Havana. There he became a center of interest. The young men became more and more interested. They began to see the superiority of the Bible doctrines to those of their accustomed teachers. One day some of them proposed to him that he meet them, and others whom they might bring, in the assembly room of the Pasaje Hotel, on Sabbath afternoon, and there tell them his experience, and what he had found in Christ. They came at the appointed time, in considerable numbers. He told them his story, and tried to show them the way of life. Some believed, some doubted; and others said: "We will hear thee again of this matter." They would come in like manner on the following Sabbath. They came, in still larger numbers, and he told them more. Then they said: "We would like to have these Sabbath meetings continued indefinitely, so that we can invite our friends and bring them under the same influence with ourselves. It is not right that we impose upon this hotel. We have no certain right to hold meetings here. Let us hire a room somewhere, and hold our meetings regularly." They went around on the other side of the same block, where they found a room, small, but large enough for their immediate requirements. From that time on, for the space of a year or more, they met regularly in the same place.

THE REFORMED CHURCH OF CUBA.

When several had come to accept the gospel and enter into the liberty that is in Christ Jesus, they desired an organization, and so called it a "Society for Religious Worship." But when it became known to the authorities that they were accustomed to hold such meetings, they were told that their assembly was contrary to law, and that they were liable to be regarded as conspirators. So they found it needful to include the word *church* in their title. They called themselves, therefore, "The Reformed Church of Cuba." This gave them government recognition, and certain legal rights and immunities which they could not have enjoyed otherwise. At the same time, the sister of Diaz, Miss Minnie, was active among the young women, and was winning one and another to the Master. Among others who believed was she who afterwards became the wife of Diaz, and whom he baptized with all her father's family.

BAPTISTS.

Soon the meetings of these people and the fact of their revolt from the Catholic Church were noised abroad, and came to the ears of certain persons from the United States, principally of the Episcopal faith. Among those who became interested was the American Consul General of the island, Mr. Ramon O. Williams, whose wife was a native of Cuba, and a member of the Catholic Church. Mr. Williams became interested so far as to subscribe to a fund to bring over to the island a representative of the Episcopal Church of the United States who might gather these people into that Church.

Soon after the subscription had been made, a priest of the Episcopal Church came to Havana. Then a bishop appeared, and, in one of the meetings, proposed that all be confirmed and become members of a Protestant Episcopal Church. Mr. Diaz could not interpose without a breach of faith with the Bible Society; and so, in compliance with the suggestion of the bishop, all kneeled down while he went around among them and "confirmed" the whole assembly. When he was gone, however, the "confirmed" came to themselves and said: "That is not what we want." Those who had already tasted of the grace of God and had passed from death to life, said : "That is too much like the Church from which we came out. Those who do not profess to have been born of the Spirit are not yet prepared for membership in a Church of Christ, a spiritual body." The others saw that the whole thing was a farce, and had no disposition to continue in such a position. But the bishop came again, and, after certain religious services, retired. Then Mr. Diaz, who had previously studied under a professor in the Union Theological Seminary in New York, and had given some attention to Church questions, while waiting for indications of the Divine will as to his service, responded to a request that he tell these neophytes wherein the principal Protestant denominations differ one from another. He told them of the bishops of the Episcopal Church, the bishopric of the Methodist Church, the presbytery of the Presbyterian Church, and the independence of the individual Baptist Church. Then he said : "All you who would like to organize as an Episcopal Church, raise your hands." Not a hand was raised. "All who would like to organize as a Methodist Church, raise your hands." Not a hand was raised. "All who would like to organize as a Presbyterian Church, raise your hands." Not a hand went up. "All who would like to organize as a Baptist Church, stand up." Every individual stood up. Then Diaz, who, like Esther, had not yet told of his denominational relations said : "I am very glad that you have expressed a preference for a Baptist Church, for I am a Baptist and will associate myself with you denominationally." Then they talked it all over, and resolved to stand together.

MARRIAGE.

Up to this time Diaz had remained unmarried; but a certain young lady among the believers had won his affections and he had received evidence that his love was reciprocated. The question of marriage had been raised. Neither of them could consent to be married by a priest of Rome, and there was no other minister on the island; and as yet civil marriages had not been recognized by the Spanish authorities. It was therefore agreed that when the Bishop should come again, as he was expected to do, they would ask him to marry them. At the beginning

of the meeting, therefore, the marriage service was performed, and the bride, according
to the custom of the country, retired with
her sister, while the bridegroom was expected
to find his way to the home of the bride at a
later hour. Diaz staid to hold the confer-
ence with his friends and with the Bishop.
At the close of the interview and after the
decision to seek union with the Baptists,
he went to his own home and went to bed.
So full was his mind of the things which he
had heard, and seen, and said, that he could
think of nothing else for half an hour, when
it suddenly occurred to him, "I was married
to-night." For a moment he was both con-
fused and amused ; rose, dressed himself
and sought the home of his bride.

A SABBATH-SCHOOL.

At the first, the work of Bro. Diaz was
mostly with young men. He had access to
very few children, and did not see his way
clear to undertake a Sabbath-school. But
his sisters, both, had been in such a school,
and they longed to see one in their own city.
They spoke to their brother about it. But
he could not see his way clear to undertake

it. One day Clotilde said: "Alberto, won't you let me be your Sabbath-school scholar? Won't you teach me, Sabbath afternoons?" Of course he said " Yes," and that was fixed. "But," said Clotilde, "Alberto, won't you let me bring——?" (naming one of her friends.) The friend came, and there was a class of two. Then said she, "Alberto, won't you let me bring——?" (naming another of her friends.) "Oh, yes; you may bring her." And soon a large class had been gathered, and before he knew it he had a full-fledged Sabbath-school. And it has been kept going from that day till now. Of course, it is not so easy to get the children of those Catholic parents as to get the children of Protestants here in our cities. But they come, and the sisters are teachers, both of them.

BAPTISMS IN THE SEA.

Meantime the Baptists of Florida had been moved to begin mission work on the island of Key West, lying on the direct route from the Western coast of that State to Havana. The Rev. W. F. Wood was sent there, and soon found in his congregation several Cubans who were working in the cigar shops, of which there are many on the island. Some of these came to him and told him of Diaz and what was going on in Cuba. Several of them gave evidence of faith in Christ, and Mr. Wood baptized them. Then they began to beseech him to go over to Havana and see for himself what was going on there. They told him that Diaz was teaching the same doctrines that he was teaching, and that he had a large following. After consulting with the Secretary of the Home Mission Board, Mr. Wood made the trip to Cuba, found Diaz, and found also that what he had heard was only part of the whole truth. He became deeply interested, and, as Diaz had not been ordained and had not presumed to baptize any one, Bro. Wood undertook to supply the lack. The little company had no baptistery, and it was contrary to law to perform such a service out of doors. Besides, there was no place within the city where baptism could be administered. But the sea was not far away, and on the north side of the city the streets run some distance from the beach. Engaging a hack Mr. Wood took two of the believers and went out along the beach, and at night, in a secluded place, left the hackman to care for his animal, while he and the believers went over the bluff, out of sight, and there he baptized them. He went again with others, and still others; but he was watched by the police, who got so near that they could take the number of the hack, though they did not recognize the men in it. They arrested the driver, the next day, and when he was brought before the magistrate and questioned as to what he had been doing, and as to the men whom he had carried, he said he did not know what was done over the bluff, but he knew that "when the men came back they were very wet." It became evident that the driver was an innocent party, and he was dismissed; but it was not safe for Bro. Wood to attempt the baptism of any others.

ORDINATION.

He encouraged Diaz to find a place where he could put a baptistery, and to come himself to Key West and receive ordination. Of course, this involved a separation from the Bible Society, and a devotement of himself entirely to the ministry of the gospel. This was decided. At that time there were

in Havana about two hundred persons of
whom Diaz, in his broken English, said
that they were "new mens and new womens."
It was this that he sought—the evidence of
regeneration. He would not put the new
wine into old bottles. He sought evidence
of a living faith and a regenerate heart.
He knew what he had received, and he
wished those who joined him to possess like
precious faith.

FIRST BAPTISM.

We have already spoken of the family of
Bro. Diaz, but only incidentally. It should
be said that his father, mother, three sisters
and a brother still remain of twenty-four
children born to their parents; and all
are in most hearty sympathy with the oldest
son and brother, the leader in the great
work of evangelization. When he began,
his work did not please his mother, who
was strongly attached to the Church of
Rome and its priesthood. For six months
she refused to speak to her son, whom
she regarded as a dangerous heretic and
a troubler of the family. After his ordination at Key West he began holding

meetings in a storeroom rented for the purpose, in which he was able to construct a
baptistery, the law not allowing any religious service or a baptism, in the open air.
During the same time, the mother, who was
mourning over the evil ways of her son, began to inquire the way of life for herself.
She could not rest, nor could she be indifferent to the things going on so near her. Yet
she made no sign till, on the night of the
first baptism in the new baptistery, what
was the amazement of the son to see his
mother in the rear of the congregation.
When the time for the baptism came, and
he was about to go into the baptistery, his
astonishment was increased, as he saw his
mother coming towards him. He thought
at first that she must be about to upbraid
him for his conduct, and tried to shun her.
But she called to him, saying, "Alberto, are
you not willing that your mother should be
a Christian and be baptized?" The surprise
was overwhelming. His heart was in his
mouth, and he hardly knew what he was
doing. Of course, he would baptize his
mother, if she believed in Jesus as her per-
sonal Savior, and repudiated the doctrines

in which she had been educated. Soon both mother and son were in the baptistery. Diaz had taken pains to commit the formula for baptism, and supposed that he could repeat it readily. But when he stood there with his mother, so much to his surprise and joy, he forgot everything but the sacred act, and lifted up his voice, saying, "O Lord Jesus, this is my mother, and I am going to baptize her." And he suited the action to the word—his first baptism, now just seven years ago. From that time his mother has been one of his most ardent supporters, her heart glowing with zeal for the work; modest, retiring, but firm and true.

A SIEGE AND A CONQUEST.

And still the father, less zealous than the mother, held to his ancestral religion. He did not forcefully or openly oppose his wife and children, but he had no sympathy with them. The years passed on and he was not converted. At length Clotilde could endure it no longer, and began to lay siege to her father's heart. One Sabbath she said to him, "Father, I have been busy this morning, and have not studied my Sabbath-school lesson as I ought to have done. Won't you read this verse for me?" Of course he would! "Oh, yes, Sis; I'll read the verse for you." And he read it. Another day she said: "Father, I have not studied my Sabbath-school lesson as much as I ought to have done, and it is late, so that I shall have to hurry to get ready for Sabbath-school. Won't you read this lesson for me while I am getting ready?" Certainly he would. And he read that lesson. And he read other lessons. After some time she said to him: "Father, I have not read my Bible as much as I ought to have done, to-day. And I'm tired and sleepy. Won't you come and sit by my bed, after I am in bed, and read the Bible to me?" Oh, yes; he would do that. So when she was in bed, he sat down by her side and began to read for her. About two o'clock in the morning, Alberto awoke and saw a light in his sister's room. He wondered what it meant, and, thinking that she might be ill, went to see. He went softly and looked in; and there sat his father, reading the Bible which he had begun to read when his daughter went to bed. Alberto returned as softly as he had come, saying, "That settles it. He'll come now." Soon he came, and now he continues steadfast in the doctrines of the Bible and the fellowship of the Baptists, one of the happiest men in Cuba, his eyes brimming with tears of joy as he sees the wonderful work of grace, and sees his whole family the fruit of it. A little child has led him.

WORK REPORTED.

In the spring of 1886, Diaz was at the meeting of the Southern Baptist Convention at Montgomery, Ala., and of his address on that occasion the JOURNAL AND MESSENGER's report said: "He gave a detailed report of his work in Havana by displaying an elaborate chart of the city. He has established a good school of sixty girls, of which his sister is principal. He has six preaching stations in Havana. If he were not careful in the reception of members, he could soon have a thousand members. At one time forty-nine asked baptism, but he told them: 'No, sir; you must read the New Testament first.' In the principal Church, all the members go with their New Testaments in their pockets, and work among the people.

Such was the earnestness and eagerness of the people that they had at one time offered $2.00 for a seat in his church. They suffered greatly from the Roman Catholics. They do not allow Protestants to be buried in their cemeteries. They will allow the interment of Jews or Chinese—anybody but Protestants. In answer to prayer, a gentleman from Boston had offered to buy a cemetery for Baptist burial. His entire family were now members of the Baptist Church. His mother was a zealous Catholic, but he was glad to say that she was the first whom he had buried with Christ in baptism. The Baptists of Havana had sent two missionaries—one to Spain and one to the United States." At that meeting our Southern brethren voted to commit the work in Cuba, although it is a foreign country, to the Home Mission Board, and began to talk about raising money for a house of worship, that the little band, which was growing too large for its quarters in the storeroom on the Prado, might have a place of worship commensurate with its needs. An Episcopalian had asked the privilege of giving $100 towards it, and the next day a Methodist lady offered a similar amount.   Diaz went back to Havana with assurances that Cuba would not be forgotten by his brethren in the United States.

THREE HUNDRED BAPTIZED.

During the first fifteen months after the organization of his Church, Diaz baptized three hundred converts, all intelligently leaving the Church of Rome and covenanting with each other to live and labor for the redemption of Cuba from the thralldom of Romanism.   They knew what they believed, and, above all, they knew why they did not longer sympathize with the Church of Rome, nor obey the behests of her priests and bishops.   Among the baptized was every member of his own family and of his wife's family, and he said: "There are seventeen of us in the house, and it is a Baptist Church."   During those fifteen months these people had given $1,078.50 for the support of their own Church ; $80 for missions in Florida, and $2 to each of the Southern Boards.   They called their organization the Gethsemane Baptist Church, after the Church in Brooklyn, N. Y., where Alberto and Minnie had been baptized. Telling of his experiences and some of the annoyances endured, in a speech before the Southern Baptist Convention, in Louisville in 1887, he said:

"Now you remember that at the last convention I told you about our cemetery; we had none. Mr. Paine, of Boston, gave me $200. I got the lot; we had to have it. They won't let us bury Baptists in consecrated ground; they are not consecrated. The Baptists have to be buried in ground with suicides and those killed by law. Before we bought our lot a member died. He was from Kentucky. We buried him, and the next day I went to put flowers on his grave. It was exposed, his coffin empty, his coat was on the ground. The priest was walking around, laughing, and said the pigs did it. I said: "You ought to take more care of the graveyard." He said it was good enough for Baptists. Then I was wicked. I went to the priest and shook him for a minute. Then I was ashamed, and asked God to forgive me, and asked the priest's pardon. He would not hear me. Oh, we had trouble there, about our cemetery! I had to write to Dr. Tichenor. Then he saw Governor Brown. He wrote to the Secretary of State, who wrote to the Cuban government, and we had no more trouble. I went to the Alabama Convention; they gave $400; that paid for it.

"When I organized the Church my mother was the first one to enter ; when I organized the cemetery, my only little daughter was the first to be buried. Oh, if the Lord will take my family as leaders, I will still praise his name. It was so bad about my daughter's death. She was playing, after getting over a sickness, on the floor ; then lay down on the bed ; her mother fanned her ; soon she screamed. I looked ; my daughter's body was there; her spirit was with the blessed Jesus. I was getting ready to come to this Convention, and did not have time to bury her. Friends brought flowers : my brother remained to bury my little daughter. My wife came with me here ; our hearts are sad, and that is why we have not accepted invitations to ride out or go to different places. I did not come to have a good time, but to tell you of God's work in Cuba."

A PROVIDENTIAL DETENTION.

At the meeting of the Southern Baptist Convention, held at Richmond, in 1888, the question of a better and larger house of worship for the Church in Havana was raised, and the Home Mission Board was instructed to expend $50,000 in the purchase of a lot and the erection of the needed house. In accordance with that vote Dr. Tichenor, the Secretary, went to Havana hoping to secure a lot which Diaz had already got his eye upon, and which he understood was for sale. But it turned out that the title could not be made good, and the Secretary, as well as Diaz, was quite disheartened. Nothing else being within reach, Dr. Tichenor decided to return home and wait for further developments. He determined to take a certain steamer, and, at the hour named for the embarkation, went down to the office to procure a ticket and go on board. Here he was met by the announcement that, in accordance with a new rule just adopted by the government, his name must be sent for a visé by an official, before he could be allowed to embark, and it was then just a moment too late to procure the visé. The list had

gone and nothing was left but to submit and
remain in Havana until the sailing of the
next steamer. Much disappointed, Dr. Tichenor returned to the hotel and he and Diaz
had another conversation over the question
of house and location. Diaz went out, and
soon returned, saying: "Doctor, I have
learned that the little theater at the corner
of Zulueta and Dragones streets is for sale.
It cost $140,000 to build it; but the owner
has failed to make it pay expenses, and it is
in the market for $70,000."

THE LAW'S DELAY.

This was a new phase of the case. The
Convention had authorized an expenditure
of $50,000, but not of $70,000. Still, there
might be propriety in considering the question. The two men sat at a certain marble-
topped table in the parlor of the hotel, over
the sidewalk. They resolved to see the
owner and make further inquiries. He came
to them, and the result was an agreement
on his part to sell them the property for
$65,000 Spanish money, the same to be paid
in three installments. The bargain was
made, subject to the ratification of the Board

of the Convention. In due time the purchase was fully authorized and the money for the first payment secured by private subscription on the part of noble-hearted men in the South. But, when it was proposed to make the payment, it was found that a good and sufficient title could not be given. The matter had to be referred to Spain, and more than a year was consumed in the perfecting of the title. But meantime, the Church was put in possession of the house, and used it as though fully owning it, without rent, beyond the interest of the purchase money. In time, however, the title was perfected and the money has now been paid, $65,000 in Spanish money, equivalent to $60,000 in American gold.

As is evident in the picture herewith, the building is not lofty. In general the public buildings of Havana are only three stories in height, and that is true of the church, which was built, as has been said, for a theatre. It will be noticed that the upper stories extend out over the side-walk, which is just within the huge pillars, or piers, prominent in the picture. There are two principal entrances, one on each street. The

lower gallery has a passage-way, or aisle,
running all the way around, behind it, and
the second, or upper gallery, extends out to
the outer wall, over the pillars. The interior
is circular, with the farther side flattened for
the stage, or pulpit platform. It is lighted
principally from the dome, seen in the cut.
There is much ornamental work around the
galleries, and the dome is panelled and
adorned with pictures and fruit scenes.
Formerly there was a series of pictures
which did not comport with the sacred use
to which the house was to be dedicated, and
they were painted out, and in their places
were put the letters spelling DIOS ES AMOR—
God is love. The rear of the stage has been
cut off, leaving only room for the baptistery
and a platform sufficient for a pulpit, running entirely across it. On the wall behind
it is the legend CUBA PARA CHRISTO—Cuba
for Christ. On either corner of the platform
is a beautiful marble pillar, the gift of a by
no means wealthy lady friend of the cause,
which serves as a support for gas fix-
tures. On the one is the letter Y and on the
other B, standing for Baptist Church. The
baptistery is a beautiful thing, in the form

GETHSEMANE BAPTIST CHURCH.

See Page 17.   HAVANA, CUBA.

of a grotto, the bottom resting on the
ground, the back built up with composite
stones and cement, artistically arranged,
with a canopy of stucco overhead and hang-
ing down as a curtain in front; wings of the
same material breaking the view on either
side in front, so that the administrator and
the candidate for baptism appear to walk
out from some other room in a grotto, and
the baptized may pass across and disappear
at the other end. It is one of the most
beautiful conceptions which we have ever
seen; and it would be quite practicable in
many other churches. It should be under-
stood that though the building appears low
in the picture, it does not produce such an
impression on one looking up at the dome
and the ceilings on the inside. It is in good
proportions every way. It is such a house
as any Church might be glad to worship
in. And it stands in the very heart of
the city, on the line between the old and
the new, only a single block from the
Prado, the principal street, and only two
blocks from the beautiful park where the
beauty and the wickedness of Havana may

be seen, any evening, in close proximity.
A line of street railroad runs before the
door.

"WAITING FOR HENNA."

The process of securing the title was long
and tedious. The house had been built on
ground formerly owned by the Spanish Government, and the progress of the matter
through the Spanish courts was attended
with the dilatoriness for which all courts
are proverbial, but which is most notable in
the courts of Spain. The money, $20,000
for the first payment, was sent over to Diaz;
but when he found out how the matter stood,
he declined to make the payment, placed the
money in bank and wrote to Dr. Tichenor,
giving him the newly discovered facts. Then
the money came back to Atlanta, and was
loaned out on call. Some who heard of it
thought that there had been mismanage-
ment, and that all was not straight. Finally,
Secretary Tichenor went over to Havana,
with the assurance that a few days would
suffice for the consummation. But still there
was delay. The owner of the property
seemed to be rather indifferent and to find

easy excuse for deferring the business. Dr.
Tichenor was taken seriously sick of fever,
and after a few days his life seemed to be in
imminent peril. He himself began to think
of the probability of his death in Cuba. One
day he said: "Diaz, if I die here, bury me
in your Cemetery, erect a little stone at my
grave and inscribe on it, 'DIED HELPING
DIAZ.'"

"No," said Diaz, "I will not say, 'Died
helping Diaz,' but 'DIED WAITING FOR
HENNA.'"

But the day of relief finally came. The
title was made good, the payment made, and
in three years the entire amount was in the
hands of the seller.

HELPERS RAISED UP.

From the time of entering the new house,
the course of the Church and pastor and his
fellow-helpers has been constantly onward.
The new believers are taught that works
must result from their faith; that they are to
make sacrifices for Christ, and are to con-
tribute according to their ability for the
spread of the gospel. The treasurer of the
church meets the candidate for baptism be-

tween the dressing room and the baptistry, and asks him how much he proposes to give for the support of the gospel. No member is retained who does not do something. Consequently there is constant progress. One mission station after another has been established, and, as a need of preachers and pastors has arisen, the Lord of the harvest has provided the men for the respective fields. While the people are, as a rule, very poor, they are far from acting the part, or presenting the appearance of paupers. They are not making appeals for help in money. Neither Diaz himself nor any of his helpers is making appeals to the people of the United States for help. They are aware that there is a great work to be done, and they do not hesitate to point it out; but when they have done that, they leave it to their brethren to determine what and how soon help is to be given.

In a little over two years after the organization of the Gethsemane Baptist Church, eleven hundred had been baptized, and Diaz said that eight thousand had offered themselves for baptism; but he was careful to receive none but those who had given evidence

of having passed from death unto life.
When he had begun to establish his out-
stations, he received a most efficient helper
in the person of the Rev. J. V. Cova, a man
of education and preaching ability, who has
been his righthand man ever since. He is in
charge of a Church known as the Pilar. At
the close of another year, in 1889, Diaz re-
ported : Missionaries, 20 ; Churches and
stations, 27 ; baptisms, 300 ; Sunday-schools,
26 ; teachers and pupils, 2,228 ; total membership of the seven Churches, 1,493; money
collected by these Churches, $2,255.70.

THE BISHOP CONFOUNDED.

It was during the year 1888-9 that the
house of worship was purchased. The issue
had been joined between the Baptists and the
Bishop of Havana. Unable to get the advantages which he desired, in the courts of the
island, the bishop went to Spain to lay the
case before the authorities at Madrid. But
the land of the Inquisition, of "Isabella the
Catholic" whose statue graces the principal
park of Havana, has undergone changes
since the days of Ferdinand, Isabella and
Alva. The laws have been so framed that

it is possible not only for Protestants to compel protection in faraway islands, but for the Baptists to carry on missions in old Spain itself, as they are doing to-day. The bishop came home discouraged, declaring in his official paper that "Alberto Diaz is the favorite of the Cuban government, which grants him privileges not conferred by the law." He had excommunicated the heretic, but the Cubans had ceased to regard the fulminations of the priesthood as they had regarded them in former days. It did not prevent Diaz from getting food and shelter and raiment as aforetime. He had the sympathy not only of the few thousands who had been in his church and had listened to his preaching, but of the people in general, even some of the Spaniards, so that he always found it practicable to get a foothold in the out-lying towns as fast as he had the men and means to occupy the ground.

THE PRIESTS AND THE CEMETERY.

But what of the opposition and resistance of the priests and the bishop? The 'only wonder is that these men have not been more determined in their persecution. Did

they know all that is involved in the issue,
they would act with even greater determina-
tion to root out the "heresay" while it is yet
young. But their day is past. It is now
too late. Diaz and his workers have found
favor with the people, and there is just
enough law on their side to give them a
certain foothold.

The first thing to be done was to secure a
place of burial for those who might die outside of the Church of Rome. The bishop
owned the only cemetery, and the only cemetery possible without the permission of the
authorities—all Romanists. The cost of
burial in the Catholic cemetery was about
$28, and it came hard on many poor people
to pay so much. The alternative was burial
in Potter's Field, in a part of the consecrated
ground, but where, after five years, the body
could be thrown out to make room for another. Of course, all shrank from that.
But for those who died Protestants there
was no hope. What should be done with
them? A cemetery became a necessity.
And so it happened, in the providence of
God, that a lot of ground directly alongside
of the bishop's cemetery was within reach,

and it was bought. When the matter became known to the authorities, no objection could be made; for the ground was just as suitable as the regular cemetery, and so they had to confirm it and allow it to be used for cemetery purposes. The first body placed in that ground was that of an old man who had been buried outside, but was disinterred and reburied. The second was the infant child of Diaz, which died and was left by him unburied, when he was obliged to take the steamer in order to reach a meeting of the Southern Baptist Convention, at Louisville, Ky., in 1887. Now there are seven thousand bodies reposing in that cemetery. But the Bishop was not to be baffled by such a strategem on the part of the heretic. He owned the ground on the hither side of the cemeteries, and between it and his cemetery ran the road which was used for both, the entrance to his being by a gate in the center of the hither side, past which the heretics had to go to get to theirs. So the bishop was seized of a bright thought. He would close up that gate and open another on the side farthest from the Protestant ground; then he would build a fence enclos-

HERRERA.   GODINEZ.   DIAZ.

IN PRISON FOR PREACHING THE GOSPEL.

See page 61.

ing all that he claimed as his, and thus he would shut the heretics out of theirs. This he did. But he did not take account of an old road which had been abandoned, but which, though in a very bad condition and hardly capable of being made passable, was yet a public highway, and could be used by the Protestants, taking them directly to their ground. By this road they now get there, but they are pretty well persuaded that the lawyers are right who tell them that the bishop has no right to close that road, and that he can yet be compelled to open it. Besides, it is held that, had our Consul General been the man he ought to have been, he could have compelled the opening of that road.

EXCOMMUNICATED.

While Diaz was absent, on one of his visits to the United States, the bishop excommunicated him, and had the fact duly advertised. To Martin Luther excommunication was no light matter, and to his friends it was a terrible blow. To a Catholic it is the most terrible thing that can befall a mortal. But it did not move Diaz. He

wrote the bishop a letter, defying his author-
ity, and proposing a public discussion in
Havana, when the people could judge for
themselves who was the heretic. Of course,
the bishop could not accept the challenge,
though the people thought that he ought to.
Diaz took advantage of the public sentiment
and gave notice, in his own congregation,
that he would discuss the questions at issue
between himself and the bishop. The announcement needed no newspaper advertis-
ing. It soon got noised abroad, and the
great Church was filled. Then the "heretic"
took up the points and handled them as the
grace of God and the Bible had taught him.
When he would rehearse the Scripture bear-
ing upon the subject, he would wind up with
the question : " Now, who is the heretic? I,
or the bishop ? " Then the hall would ring
with applause which meant, The bishop is
the heretic. And thus a triumph was gained.

HELPFUL FRIENDS.

Spanish law, with regard to religious meetings, is peculiar, and, under the inspiration
of the priests, it is quite likely to be en-
forced. Diaz not only knew the law, but he

had a good friend in Signor Charmat, to help him in an emergency. The law requires that one who would hold a religious service outside of the Church shall give notice in writing as to the time and place of such assembly. On one occasion, in June, 1890, Diaz and two of his helpers, Godinez and Herrera, and a large number of his congregation, went out to the little city, Guanabacoa, the birth place of Diaz, where they had been accustomed to hold meetings for six months, Bro. Herrera being the pastor in charge. Before the close of the meeting the three men were arrested and taken before the mayor of the city, who claimed that no notice of the meeting had been given, and ordered them locked up in the common jail. They went quietly, but were followed by a great throng of people, all greatly excited and indignant over the treatment of the preachers. Infuriated and ready to mob the officers in charge, they surrounded the prison, and Diaz was compelled to appear on the balcony and dissuade them from attempting his rescue. Nineteen hours after, the original notice was found in the office of the mayor, and in order to shield himself and his officers for the outrage upon the prisoners, he claimed that there was a word omitted in the notice, the name of the person who was to conduct the service ; and that, though the name of Herrera was signed to it. But the men remained in prison for two days and a half.

Diaz is an American citizen, and, of course the outrage gave him a claim for protection by our government. His imprisonment was immediately telegraphed to Dr. Tichenor, and as speedily to Mr. Blaine, then Secretary of State. Mr. Blaine acted promptly and demanded the release of Diaz, and an accounting for his imprisonment. But our Consul General trifled with the matter, and brought down upon him the indignation of the friends of Diaz and of liberty, both in Cuba and in the United States. When Mr. Porta, one of Diaz's helpers, went to Mr. Williams about it, he said, petulantly: "These Baptists are always making me trouble," and he did not hurry to help them. Mr. Williams is an old man, and his services in Havana will doubtless terminate soon. We have already intimated the point upon which, as he said to the writer, he "did not

agree with Mr. Diaz." The picture pre-
sented herewith shows Diaz and the two
brethren in prison, a photograph having
been taken while they were there. They
had never been so popular in Cuba as they
were when they came out of that prison

NEED OF SCHOOLS

His sisters, Minnie and Clotilde, had
been his helpers from the first, and a year
or two later the latter came over to Georgia
and spent some time in a Baptist school, the
better fitting herself for work of a high
order. It has begun to be felt that the next
step in the evangelization of the island, and
for holding securely what has been already
achieved, is a high school for girls. Such a
school has been carried on for two or three
years, but under great disadvantages. Now
the time seems to have come for something
more permanent and more attractive to the
people. There are in Havana many families,
not yet Protestant, which would gladly place
their daughters under the care of these
young ladies, provided the accommodations
were such that they could be made comfort-
able. The customs of the city and country

do not admit of a young woman's walking in the street unattended. If she would have the advantages of such a school as is contemplated, she must go to it and remain during the entire week, unless some member of her family can attend her both in coming and going. There are families of wealth who want their daughters to learn English and to pursue their studies in English text-books, and these are willing to pay good prices for such tuition; but in order to secure these as pupils, there must be a house of sufficient size, and with such appurtenances, that the young women can become boarders and remain during the week, or during the term.

To the securement of such a home for a school, attention has now been turned, and the place seems to have been prepared for it by Providence. A theater building, directly across the street from the Gethsemane church, is for sale at a low figure. A few thousand dollars would adapt it to the requirements of a school, and the lot is so large and is so secluded from the public gaze, by virtue of a breast wall, an iron fence and shade trees, that it seems to have been fitted up for just such a purpose. The property could have been bought cheap, when we were there, and we hope to hear that it has been secured.

We have given this account of the "Apostle of Cuba" and the work going on there, in order that those who read it may become intelligent witnesses of the displays of divine grace and power in this last quarter of the nineteenth century. Great things are in progress in foreign lands. The reports coming up from our mission fields in Europe, Asia and Africa are most encouraging and inspiring. France, in particular, is just now the scene of wonderful displays of grace, in connection with our Baptist missions, and something like what has been going on in Cuba is going on in different parts of France. In Toulon a whole Church has been admitted to baptism. The work of our Southern brethren in Cuba is paralleled only by what is doing among the missions of the Missionary Union in the far away lands. The fathers have sown, and we are reaping the fruits of their sowing. The gospel is winning its way, notwithstanding the efforts of the infidels and the half-and-half Christians(?) to throw doubt over the sacred word and undermine the faith of the elect. The Lord God omnipotent reigneth, and he is getting to himself a name, and the nations are his witnesses. It is ours to bear some humble part in the achievement of the triumph.